FUN
WITH
RIDDLES

By the same author

Little Red Book Series

A2Z Book Series

Others

FUN WITH RIDDLES

TERRY O'BRIEN

RUPA

Published by
Rupa Publications India Pvt. Ltd 2013
7/16, Ansari Road, Daryaganj
New Delhi 110002

Sales centres:

Allahabad Bengaluru Chennai
Hyderabad Jaipur Kathmandu
Kolkata Mumbai

ISBN: 978-81-291-2384-8

10 9 8 7 6 5 4 3 2 1

The moral right of the author has been asserted.

Typeset in Times New Roman 10/12
by Innovative Processors, New Delhi

Printed at Repro Knowledgecast Limited, Thane

Acknowledgement

*A special thanks to Allen O'Brien, my son,
who assisted me in having fun while
compiling and re-imagining what's
essential for such a book*

PREFACE

Most of us love riddles and puzzles. They give us the opportunity for out of the box thinking; besides fun they rattle our brains. They are a good way to pass the time when we are alone. They come of use when we want to have fun thinking; playing with some brain teasers.

Apart from being entertaining, riddles are also very good for the development of our mind. Solving riddles also stimulates the brain and reduces chances of memory loss later. Riddles are like 'Tonic for the Mind'.

Riddles and brain teasers are a great way to get a good laugh! Thousands of years ago, people just like us were interested in a good riddle or puzzle. One of the first uses for a riddle was to "secretly" carry a message from one person to another — It was a quiz of sorts that only you knew the answer to, and hopefully the person on the other end would be smart enough to solve or figure out.

Probably the biggest brain teaser is trying to solve the puzzle of the mind itself. Understanding how our brains work has been one of the greatest mysteries ever. Today, the workings of the brain are still a riddle or brain teaser in need of a solution, if you are interested.

Fun with Riddles would be a wonderful place for you to start warming up for a mental challenge. Almost everyone loves a good mystery or puzzle, and riddles are a fun way of exercising your brain and testing your friends' skills as well. Best of all, riddles and brain teasers are there to be enjoyed. So, prepare to be tricked, tested, riddled, and teased until you can't but give it up. This book would be a wonderful place for you to start warming up for a mental challenge.

Happy Reading!

Riddle No. 1

There are two Indians: a big Indian, and a little Indian. The little Indian is the big Indian's son, but the big Indian is not the little Indian's father. How is this possible?

Riddle No. 2

If it takes twenty minutes to hard-boil one goose egg, how long will it take to hard-boil four goose eggs?

Riddle No. 3

Some months have 31 days. How many of them have 28 days?

Riddle No. 4

Can a man in India marry his widow's sister?

Riddle No. 5

Take the number 30, divide it by 1/2, and then add 10. What do you get?

Riddle No. 6

A doctor gives you three pills and tells you to take one every half an hour. How long will the pills last?

Riddle No. 7

Two spies want to get into an enemy's military base. In order to get in they have to give the correct countersign to the guard at the gate after he gives them the sign. They wait hiding near the gate so that they can overhear the countersign from another soldier.

One soldier comes and the guard gives the sign: '6'. The soldier answers '3'. The guard lets him pass. Another soldier comes.The guard says '12' and the soldier gives the answer '6'. The guard lets him pass. So, the first spy goes to the gate and the guard says '10'.The spy, sure that he knew the answer, says '5'. Immediately, the guard shoots him dead.

Then the second spy, who saw the previous spy being killed when he gave the countersign, had now understood what the right answer would be, whatever the guard's sign was. So, he walks to the gate and the guard says '8'. The spy gives the correct answer and the guard lets him in. What was the answer that the spy gave?

Riddle No. 8

Einstein wrote this quiz last century. He said that 98% of the people in the world cannot solve the quiz.

There are 5 houses in 5 different colours

In each house lives a person with a different nationality

These 5 owners drink a certain type of beverage, smoke a certain brand of cigar, and keep a certain pet

No owners have the same pet, smoke the same brand of cigar or drink the same drink

Here's the question: Who owns the fish?

The Brit lives in a red house

The Swede keeps dogs as pets

The Dane drinks tea

The green house is on the left of the white house

The green house owner drinks coffee

The person who smokes Pall Mall rears birds

The owner of the yellow house smokes Dunhill

The man living in the house right in the middle drinks milk

The Norwegian lives in the first house

The man who smokes Blend lives next door to the one who keeps cats.

The man who keeps horses lives next door to the man who smokes Dunhill

The owner who smokes Blue Master drinks beer

The German smokes Prince

The Norwegian lives next to the blue house

The man who smokes Blend has a neighbour who drinks water

With these 15 clues the problem is solvable.

Riddle No. 9

A man was at a bar feeling poor. He sees a rich man take ₹1000 out of his pocket to pay the cashier. The poor man says to the rich man, 'I know all the songs known to man.' The rich man laughed and said, 'I bet you all the money in my pocket that you can't sing a song with my daughter's name in it, Purnima.' The poor man went home richer and the rich man went home poorer. What song did the man sing?

Riddle No. 10

Nutan's husband's father-in-law is Nutan's husband's brother's brother-in-law, and Nutan's sister-in-law is Nutan's brother's stepmother. How did this happen?

Riddle No. 11

A sparrow has fallen into a hole in a rock. The hole measures three inches in diameter and is three feet deep. Due to the depth of the hole, the sparrow cannot be reached by hand. We cannot use sticks or canes because we could hurt the bird. How can you get the bird out?

Riddle No. 12

A ribbon is 30 inches long. If you cut it with a pair of scissors into one-inch pieces, how many snips would it take?

Riddle No. 13

A man worked at a high security institution. The man tried to log into his computer, but the computer denied the password. He then remembered that the passwords to the computers were reset every month for security reasons. He called his boss for his new password.

The man said, 'Boss, my old password is out of date.'

The boss said, 'Yes, it is. The new password is different, but if you listen closely you will be able to figure out the new one. Your new password has the same amount of letters as the old one, and four of the letters are the same.'

The man then logged into his computer with no trouble; what was the new password? What was his old password?

Riddle No. 14

A bus driver was heading down a street in Chandigarh. He went right past a stop sign without stopping. He turned left where there was a 'no left turn' sign and he took the wrong way on a one-way street. Then he went on the left side of the road past a police patrol car. Still - he didn't break any traffic laws. Why not?

Riddle No. 15

What common English word will describe a person or thing as not being found in any place and yet with no changes other than a space between syllables, will correctly describe that person or thing as being actually present at this very moment?

Riddle No. 16

A woman shoots her husband.

Then she holds him under water for over 5 minutes.

Finally, she hangs him.

But 5 minutes later they both go out together and enjoy a wonderful dinner together.

How can this be?

Riddle No. 17

One night, a man receives a call from the Police. The Police tells the man that his wife was murdered, and that he should reach the crime scene as soon as possible. The man drops the phone, shocked, and reaches the crime scene within 20 minutes. As soon as he reaches the crime scene, the police arrest him, and he is convicted of murder. How did the police know that he committed the crime?

Riddle No. 18

As I went across the bridge, I met a man with a load of wood, which was neither straight nor crooked. What kind of wood was it?

Riddle No. 19

I am a three digit number.
My tens digit is five more than my ones digit.
My hundreds digit is eight less than my tens digit.
What number am I?

Riddle No. 20

What belongs to you, but others use it more than you do?

Riddle No. 21

We are very little creatures; all of us have different features. One of us in glass is set; one of us you'll find in jet. Another you may see in tin, and a fourth is boxed within. If the fifth you should pursue, it can never fly from you.

Riddle No. 22

I am the centre of gravity. I hold a capital situation in Vienna, and as I am foremost in every victory, am allowed by all to be invaluable. Though I am invisible, I am clearly seen in the midst of a river. I could name three who are in love with me and have three associates in vice. It is in vain that you seek me for I have long been in heaven yet even now lie embalmed in the grave. What am I?

Riddle No. 23

Before any changes I'm a garlic or spice. My first is altered and I'm a hand-warming device. My second is changed and I'm trees in full bloom. The next letter change makes a deathly old tomb. Change the fourth to make a fruit of the vine. Change the last for a chart plotted with lines. What was I? What did I become? What did I turn out to be?

Riddle No. 24

Why is it against the law for a man living in Delhi to be buried in Mumbai?

Riddle No. 25

Four of us are in your field,
But our differences keep us at yield.
First, a one that is no fool,
Though he resembles a gardener's tool.
Next, one difficult to split in two,
And a girl once had one as big as her shoe.
Then, to the mind, one's a lovely bonder,
And truancy makes it grow fonder.
Last, a stem connecting dots of three,
Knowing all this, what are we?

Riddle No. 26

Why was the math book sad?

Riddle No. 27

In a stable there are men and horses. In all there are 22 heads and 72 feet. How many men and how many horses are in the stable.

Riddle No. 28

$26 + 78 + 39 = 1,318,311,415$
$33 + 28 + 49 = 2,612,131,217$
$92 + 43 + 10 = 1124$
$11 + 60 + 3 = ?$
What is the answer and why?
HINT: It's only 2 numbers.

Riddle No. 29

A boy is stuck on a deserted island. There is a bridge to connect the island to the mainland. Halfway across the bridge, there is a guard. The guard will not let anyone from the mainland to the island, or anyone from the island to the mainland. If the guard catches someone, he sends him or her back. The guard sleeps for 30 seconds and then is awake for 5 minutes. The island is surrounded by man-eating sharks, and the boy does not have anything with him except for his own shirt and his pants. It takes the boy 1 minute to cross the bridge. How does he cross the bridge without getting caught?

Riddle No. 30

Jatin is 12 years old, Satish is 12 years old. After 5 years Jatin turns 17 years old and Satish turns 18 years. How could that be?

Riddle No. 31

A man accidentally fell in a 30 metres high well. His friend gave him a rope. The man was able to climb 3 metres, but slipped back 2 metres in 5 minutes.

How much time will he take to climb up the well?

Riddle No. 32

You are killed in a plane crash and find yourself at 2 doors: one leads to heaven and the other to hell. There is a troll at each door and the trolls are identical in every way. You find instructions posted on the wall behind you: you can ask one question and one question only, and you can only direct it to one of the trolls. One troll will always lie to you regardless of your question, and the other will always tell you the truth. Only the trolls themselves know which will lie and which will be truthful, and that is all you are told. What one question should you ask?

Riddle No. 33

LOL. $101 \times 5 = 505$ which looks like SOS.

$567 \times 2 = 01134$ (type this in a calculator and turn upside down) looks like hello.

$101 \times 7 = 707$ turn upside down and it becomes LOL.

Riddle No. 34

I have a glass of water. I pour it into a bigger glass of water and it fills completely to the top. I pour that same amount of water into another bigger glass of water and it reaches the top, and I repeat this process again 3 more times. How is this possible?

Riddle No. 35

Three friends check into a motel for the night and the clerk tells them the bill is ₹3000, payable in advance. So, they each pay the clerk ₹1000 and go to their room. A few minutes later, the clerk realises he has made an error and overcharged the trio by ₹500. He asks the Assistant to return ₹500 to the 3 friends who had just checked in. The Assistant sees this as an opportunity to make ₹200 as he reasons that the three friends would have a tough time dividing ₹500 evenly among them; so he decides to tell them that the clerk made a mistake of only ₹300, giving a hundred rupee note back to each of the friends. He pockets the leftover ₹200 and goes home for the day! Now, each of the three friends gets a hundred rupee back, thus they each paid ₹900 for the room, which is a total of ₹2700 for the night. We know the Assistant pocketed ₹200 and adding that to the ₹2,700, you get ₹2,900, not ₹3,000 which was originally spent. Where did the other hundred rupees go????

Riddle No. 36

You have two slow-burning fuses, each of which will burn up in exactly one hour. They are not necessarily of the same length and width as each other, nor even necessarily of uniform width, so you can't measure a half hour by noting when one fuse is half burned. Using these two fuses, how can you measure 45 minutes?

Riddle No. 37

1=3

2=3

3=5

4=4

5=4

So what does...

6=

7=

Riddle No. 38

What does hEllO times hI equal?

Riddle No. 39

I'm a four-digit number! My 2nd digit is twice greater than my 3rd. The sum of all my digits is thrice greater than my last digit! The product of my 3rd and 4th digits is 12 times greater than the ratio of my 2nd to 3rd. What am I?

Riddle No. 40

Three men eat dinner in a restaurant. The bill is ₹2,500. They each put in ₹1,000. The waiter brings back five one hundred rupee notes. They give the waiter a tip ₹200 and keep ₹100 each. So now each person spent ₹900. If 300x9 = ₹2,700, plus ₹200 for tip = ₹2,900, where did the other hundred rupee go?

Riddle No. 41

Horse A can run 1 lap per minute.

Horse B can run 2 laps per minute.

Horse C can run 4 laps per minute.

If they all start at the same time at the same place, how much long will it take for each of them to meet back at the starting line?

Riddle No. 42

Look at a digital clock. How many times will the clock show 3 or more consecutive numbers?

Riddle No. 43

Rohit wishes to get into a club. He knows that the club requires a code. He stands around the corner and listens to two people get past the bouncer.

The bouncer tells Pradeep to de-code six, Pradeep reply's with three and gets in.

The bouncer then tells Funtoosh to de-code Twelve, Funtoosh reply's with six and gets in.

Right now Rohit is quite confident that he can get in, he walks to the bouncer and is told to de-code ten. Rohit happily replies with five, but is not let in.

What is the number he should have said to get in and how do you de-code it?

Riddle No. 44

Tall, tall man,
Bushy, bushy hair,
Balls hanging!
Who or what is this?

Riddle No. 45

There are five dacoits, A, B, C, D and E. They find 100 gold coins. They must decide how to distribute them. The dacoits have a strict order of seniority: A is superior to B, who is superior to C, who is superior to D, who is superior to E.

The dacoits also follow strict rules of coin distribution, which are thus: the most senior dacoits should propose a distribution of coins. The dacoits, including the senior dacoit, then vote on whether to accept this distribution. If the proposed allocation is accepted by a majority vote, it happens. If not, the proposer is SHOT DEAD AND DIES, and the next most-senior dacoit makes a new proposal to begin the system again.

In the event of a tie vote, the most senior dacoit has the casting vote.

Dacoits base their decisions on three factors, in order of priority:

First, each dacoit wants to survive.

Second, each dacoit wants to maximize the number of gold coins he receives.

Third, all things being equal the dacoits would prefer to shoot the most senior dacoits.

Determine the number of coins each dacoit receives.

Riddle No. 46

6 is 3, 3 is 5, 5 is 4, 4 is cosmic. Why is 4 cosmic?

Riddle No. 47

49 + 7 = RUN
6 + 85 = CAT
5 + 76 + 16 = BOSS
So, 35 + 33 + 16 = ?

Riddle No. 48

What row of numbers comes next in this series?
1
11
21
1211
111221
312211
13112221

Riddle No. 49

You have a barrel of oil, and you need to measure out just one gallon. How do you do this if you only have a three-gallon container and a five-gallon container?

Riddle No. 50

Arnold Schwarzenegger has a big one
Michael J Fox has a small one
Madonna doesn't have one
The Pope has one, but he never uses it
Bill Clinton has one and he uses it all the time!
What is it?

Riddle No. 51

If your sock drawer has 6 black socks, 4 brown socks, 8 white socks, and 2 tan socks, how many socks would you have to pull out in the dark to be sure you had a matching pair?

Riddle No. 52

A large truck is crossing a bridge 1 mile long. The bridge can only hold 14000 lbs, which is the exact weight of the truck. The truck makes it half way across the bridge and stops. A bird lands on the truck. Does the bridge collapse? Give a reason.

Riddle No. 53

Mom and Dad have four daughters, and each daughter has one brother. How many people are there in the family?

Riddle No. 54

What English word retains the same pronunciation, even after you take away four of its five letters?

Riddle No. 55

Why wasn't Sandy put in jail after killing dozens of people?

Riddle No. 56

If I say "Everything I tell you is a lie," am I telling you the truth or a lie?

Riddle No. 57

The paragraph below is very unusual. How quickly can you find out what is so unusual about it?

[The passage is taken from the book *Gatsby* written by Ernest Vincent Wright in the late 1930s.]

'Gatsby was walking back from a visit down in Branton Hill's manufacturing district on a Saturday night. A busy day's traffic had its noisy run; and with not many folks in sight, His Honour got along without having to stop to grasp a hand, or talk; for a mayor out of City Hall is a shining mark for any politician. And so, coming to Broadway, a booming bass drum and sounds of singing, told of a small Salvation Army unit carrying on amidst Broadway's night shopping crowds. Gatsby walking towards that group, saw a young girl, back toward him, just finishing a long, soulful oration ...'

Riddle No. 58

While exploring the wild, Vikram was captured by goblins. Betaal, the chief of the goblins told him he was allowed one final statement on which would hinge how he would die. If the statement he made was false, he would be boiled in water. If the statement were true, he would be fried in oil. Since Vikram did not like either option, so he made a statement that forced the goblins to release him. What is the one statement he could make to save himself?

Riddle No. 59

You have a jug of milk, and you need to measure out just one cup. How do you do this if you only have a three-cup measuring container and a five-cup container?

Riddle No. 60

The ages of a father and son add up to 66. The father's age is the son's age reversed. How old could they be?

Riddle No. 61

A man is on a trip with a lion, a goat and a stack of leaves. He comes upon a stream, which he has to cross, and finds a tiny boat which he can use for the same. The problem though, is that he can only take himself and either the lion, the goat, or the stack of leaves across at a time. It is not possible for him to leave the lion alone with the goat or the goat alone with the stack of leaves. How can he get all safely over the stream?

Riddle No. 62

You are standing in front of a room with one light bulb inside of it. You cannot see if it is on or off. Outside the room there are 3 switches in the off positions. You may turn the switches any way you want to. You stop turning the switches, enter the room and know which switch controls the light bulb. How?

Riddle No. 63

A boy was at a carnival and went to a booth where a man said to the boy, 'If I write your exact weight on this piece of paper then you have to give me ₹50, but if I cannot, I will pay you ₹ 50.' The boy looked around and saw no scale so he agrees thinking no matter what the machine writes he'll just say he weighs more or less. In the end the boy ended up paying the man ₹50. How did the man win the bet?

Riddle No. 64

After teaching his class all about Roman numerals (X = 10, IX = 9 and so on) the teacher asked his class to draw a single continuous line and turn IX into 6. The only stipulation the teacher made was that the pen could not be lifted from the paper until the line was complete.

Riddle No. 65

What's smaller than an ant's mouth?

Riddle No. 66

How can you drop a raw egg onto a concrete floor without cracking it?

Riddle No. 67

Two mothers and two daughters go to a pet store and buy three cats. Each female gets her own cat. How is this possible?

Riddle No. 68

There are 3 stoves: A glass stove, a brick stove and a wood stove. You only have 1 match. Which do you light up first?

Riddle No. 69

How far can a dog run into the woods?

Riddle No. 70

I turn polar bears white
And I will make you cry.
I make guys have to pee
And girls comb their hair.
I make celebrities look stupid
And normal people look like celebrities.
I turn pancakes brown
And make your champagne bubble.
If you squeeze me, I'll pop.
If you look at me, you'll pop.
Can you answer this riddle?

Riddle No. 71

The following number is the only one of its kind: 8,549,176,320. Can you figure out what is so special about it?

Riddle No. 72

What are the next two letters in the following series and why?

W A T N T L I T F S _ _?

Riddle No. 73

If you wrote all the numbers from 300 to 400 on a piece of paper, how many times would you have written the number 3?

Riddle No. 74

Two vertical 750 ft posts have 1000 ft rope stretched between their top most points. The rope sags to within 250 ft from the ground. How far apart are the posts?

Riddle No. 75

A murderer is condemned to death. He has to choose between three rooms. The first is full of raging fires, the second is full of assassins with loaded guns and the third is full of lions that haven't eaten in 3 years. Which room is safest for him?

Riddle No. 76

I have two arms, but fingers none. I have two feet, but cannot run. I carry well, but I have found I carry best with my feet off the ground. What am I?

Riddle No. 77

You are in a place called MAGIC WORLD and there is only one law. There is a mirror, but no reflection. There is pizza with cheese, but no sausage. There is pepper, but no salt. There is a door, yet no entrance or exit. What is the law?

Riddle No. 78

I am strongest when you see me as round, but I am often viewed in other forms. I lift and drop the sea with my tremendous strength, and a man with a name like 'powerful bicep' was the first to tread on me. What am I?

Riddle No. 79

Rearrange the letters in the word, 'new door', to make one word.

Riddle No. 80

Which is correct to say, 'The yolk of the egg are white' or 'The yolk of the egg is white'?

Riddle No. 81

What three letter word can prefix the following three words to make three new words? Ache, Nest and Drum.

Riddle No. 82

If you toss a dice and it comes up with the number one 9 times in a row, what is the probability that it will come up with one on the next throw?

Riddle No. 83

Look at me. I can bring a smile to your face, a tear to your eye, or even a thought to your mind. But, I can't be seen. What am I?

Riddle No. 84

Farmer Hari Prasad owns three white cows, four brown cows and one black cow. How many of Hari Prasad's cows are the same colour as another cow on Hari Prasad's farm?

Riddle No. 85

Can you name three consecutive days without using the words Monday, Tuesday, Wednesday, Thursday, Friday, Saturday or Sunday?

Riddle No. 86

Rahul has parked his car in a mall. On the left read 16, 06, 68, 88. One the right 98 which spot did he park in?

Riddle No. 87

The word has seven letters. It preceded God. It is greater than God, is more evil than the devil, poor people have it, rich people need it and if you eat it, you will die. What is it?

Riddle No. 88

I turn polar bears white
And I will make you cry.
I make guys have to pee
And girls comb their hair.
I make celebrities look stupid
And normal people look like celebrities.
I turn pancakes brown
And make your champagne bubble.
If you squeeze me, I'll pop.
If you look at me, you'll pop.
Can you answer this riddle?

Riddle No. 89

A man is travelling to a town and comes to a fork in the road. If he goes left, he goes to the Liars' village. If he goes right, he then goes to the village of Truths - which is where he wants to go. However, he does not know which way is which. He doesn't have time to take both routes, so he approaches a stranger who is standing in the middle of the fork. The stranger says he may only ask 3 questions and he will answer them. The man asks, 'Are you from the village of Truths?' The stranger says, 'Yes!' However, the man is still facing a dilemma: If the stranger was from the village of Truths he can only tell the truth, but if he was from the village of Liars, he would say he was from the village of Truth. So then he asks the stranger: 'Are you telling the truth?' The stranger says, 'Yes!' But sadly this leaves the man in the same position as before. Can you figure it out ?

Riddle No. 90

These two words are synonyms when applied to one's career, but are antonyms when applied to the same person's character?

Riddle No. 91

If a chicken says, 'All Chickens are liars', is the chicken telling the truth?

Riddle No. 92

A man dies of thirst in his own home. How is this possible?

Riddle No. 93

I have a head and tail, but no body. What am I?

Riddle No. 94

I am, in truth, a yellow fork
From tables in the sky
By inadvertent fingers dropped
The awful cutlery.
Of mansions never quite disclosed
And never quite concealed
The apparatus of the dark
To ignorance revealed.

– *Emily Dickenson*

Riddle No. 95

Think of words ending in –GRY: Angry and hungry are two of them. There are only three words in the English language. What is the third word? The word is something that everyone uses every day. If you have listened carefully, I have already told you what it is.

Riddle No. 96

The person who makes it, sells it. The person who buys it never uses it and the person who uses it doesn't know what they are. What is it?

Riddle No. 97

Which English word has three consecutive double letters?

Riddle No. 98

What's black when you get it, red when you use it, and white when you're all through with it?

Riddle No. 99

I am always hungry,
I must always be fed,
The finger I touch,
Will soon turn red.

Riddle No. 100

I have four legs, but no tail. Usually I am heard only at night. What am I?

Riddle No. 101

This is a thirteen-letter word that has the same vowel at least 4 times and has only 3 other consonants?

Riddle No. 102

What happened in 1961 that will not happen again for over 4000 years?

Riddle No. 103

What is it that no man ever saw, which never was, but always will be?

Riddle No. 104

What 3 letters change a girl into a woman?

Riddle No. 105

A woman owns a shop and the first day she had 13 customers, the second day she had 14 customers, the third 95 and the fourth 62. Following the sequence, how many customers will she have tomorrow?

Riddle No. 106

Which ten-letter word can be formed using only the first line of your computer keyboard → QWERTYUIOP?

Riddle No. 107

I never was, am always to be, no one ever saw me, nor ever will. And yet I am the confidence of all who live and breathe on this terrestrial ball. What am I?

Riddle No. 108

I was a long white petticoat
And red cup
The longer I wear the cup
The shorter it grows!

Riddle No. 109

One by one we fall from heaven
down into the depths of the past
And our world is ever upturned
so that yet some time we'll last

Riddle No. 110

I drift forever with the current,
Down these long canals they've made.
Tame, yet wild, I run elusive,
Multi-tasking to your aid.
Before I came, the world was darker,
Colder, sometimes, rougher, true.
But though I might make living easy,
I'm good at killing people too.

Riddle No. 111

Reaching stiffly for the sky,
I bare my fingers when it's cold.
In warmth I wear an emerald glove,
And in between I dress in gold.

Riddle No. 112

Kings and queens may cling to power,
and the jester's got his call.
But, as you may all discover,
the common one outranks them all.

Riddle No. 113

Every dawn begins with me,
At dusk I'll be the first you see.
And daybreak couldn't come without,
What midday centres all about.
Daises grow from me, I'm told,
And when I come, I end all cold.
But in the sun I won't be found,
Yet still, each day I'll be around.

Riddle No. 114

Kings and lords and Christians raised them,
Since they stand for higher powers.
Yet few of them would stand, I'm certain,
If women ruled this world of ours.

Riddle No. 115

Soft and fragile is my skin,
I get my growth in mud.
I'm dangerous as much as pretty,
For if not careful, I draw blood.

Riddle No. 116

Three brothers share a family sport:
A non-stop marathon;
The oldest one is fat and short,
And trudges slowly on.
The middle brother's tall and slim,
And keeps a steady pace.
The youngest runs just like the wind,
A-speeding through the race.
'He's young in years, we let him run,'
The other brothers say,
'Cause though he's surely number one,
He's second, in a way.'

Riddle No. 117

It's true I bring serenity,
And hang around the stars.
But yet I live in misery;
You'll find me behind bars.
With thieves and villains I consort,
In prison I'll be found.
But I would never go to court,
Unless there's more than one.

Riddle No. 118

There once was a strange man who loved wordplay, he had a very important and successful business that would take insect shipments from all across the world and distribute them to zoos across the US.What was the name of his company?

Riddle No. 119

There is one word that stands the test of time and holds fast to the centre of everything. Though everyone will try at least once in their life to move around this word, but in fact, unknowingly, they use it every moment of the day. Young or old, awake or in sleep, human or animal, this word stands fast. It belongs to everyone, to all living things, but no one can master it. The word is?

Riddle No. 120

My days are in the summer,
When you'll eat me when I'm hot.
In fact I'll even eat myself,
Where battles tough are fought.
But when you find me in a fight,
'Twill be high in the sky.
And if you catch me napping.

I suggest you let me lie,
When you're bad come to my house.
From Ma get thoughts profound,
Am I big or am I small?
Some say I'm just a pound.

Riddle No. 121

Friday = 63
Sunday = 84
What day of the week = 100?

Riddle No. 122

A mile from end to end, yet as close to as a friend: A precious
commodity, freely given: Seen on the dead and on the living.
Found on the rich, poor, short and tall, but shared among
children most of all. What is it?

Riddle No. 123

Four of us are in your field,
But our differences keep us at yield.
First, a one that is no fool,

Though he resembles a gardener's tool.
Next, one difficult to split in two,
And a girl once had one as big as her shoe.
Then, to the mind, one's a lovely bonder,
And truancy makes it grow fonder.
Last, a stem connecting dots of three,
Knowing all this, what are we?

Riddle No. 124

It's red, blue, purple and green, no one can reach it, not even the queen. What is it?

Riddle No. 125

I am a word of meanings three.
Three ways of spelling me there be.
The first is an odour, a smell if you will.
The second some money, but not in a bill.
The third is past tense, a method of passing things on or around.
Can you tell me now, what these words are, that have the same sound?

Riddle No. 126

I am a word of 5 letters and people eat me. If you remove the first letter I become a form of energy. Remove the first two and I'm needed to live. Scramble the last 3 and you can drink me. What am I?

Riddle No. 127

Most plural words in English have an 'S' right in the end. What is the word, when containing an 'S' in the end, not only become plural, but also changes gender?

Riddle No. 128

Alone I am hot. Take two letters away and I am cold. Take another away and I warm up a bit. What all am I?

Riddle No. 129

Alive without breath,
As cold as death,
Clad in mail never clinking,
Never thirsty, ever drinking.

Riddle No. 130

What has roots that nobody sees,
Is taller than trees,
Up, up it goes,
Yet it never grows?

Riddle No. 131

A man rides into town on Friday, stays for three days and leaves on Friday. How did he do it?

Riddle No. 132

It cannot be seen, it cannot be felt,
Cannot be heard, cannot be smelt,
Lies behind stars and under hills,
And empty holes it fills.
Comes first follows after,
Ends life kills laughter.

Riddle No. 133

An eye in a blue face
Saw an eye in a green face.
'That eye is like this eye'
Said the first eye,
But in a low, not high place.

Riddle No. 134

Anjali always lies, while Neha always speaks the truth. One said, 'The other one says he is Anjali.' Who said that?

Riddle No. 135

The first 2 letters of this English word refer to a male, the first three refer to a female, the first 4 to a great man and the whole word is a great woman. What is the word?

Riddle No. 136

I met an old man on London bridge,
As the sun set on the ridge,
He tipped his hat and drew his name,
And cheated at the guessing game.
What was the man's name?

Riddle No. 137

yyyy U R, yyyy U B, I C U R y y 4 ?
Which word belongs in place of the question mark?

Riddle No. 138

I'm not the sort that's eaten, I'm not the sort you bake,
Don't put me in an oven, I don't taste that great,
But when applied correctly, around me you will find,
Problems are so simple when my digits come to mind.

Riddle No. 139

This walks on graves at night yet in homes during the day,
Men are scared of it, women like it, children play with it,
It lives on dates and salt,
It is covered in hair,
Its name starts with 'M' and it is mentioned in the Quran.
What is it?

Riddle No. 140

We are four against the masses. We are trying to find the
one who is the whole package. We sigh, we laugh, we frown
while we hope that the next one will be the one. Who are
we?

Riddle No. 141

I'm up and down and round about,
yet all the world can't find me out.
Though thousands have employed their leisure,
they never yet could find my measure.
I'm found in almost every garden,
In a compass or a fardel.
There's neither chariot coach nor mill
may move one inch except I will.
What am I?

Riddle No. 142

Comes as wooden as a tree,
Covered in paint, don't you see,
Makes you laugh, or run and hide,
For it has something dark inside.

Riddle No. 143

How can you add eight to get the number 1,000? (only use addition)

Riddle No. 144

What is the missing number in the order?
2, 49, 36, 18, 8.

Riddle No. 145

Two fathers and two sons sat down to eat eggs for breakfast. They ate exactly three eggs, each person had an egg. The Riddle is for you to explain how.

Riddle No. 146

A merchant can place 8 large boxes or 10 small boxes into a carton for shipping. In one shipment, he sent a total of 96 boxes. If there are more large boxes than small boxes, how many cartons did he ship?

Riddle No. 147

What starts with 'P' ends with 'E' and has a million letters in it?

Riddle No. 148

Three brothers live in a farm. They agreed to buy new seeds: Raj and Om Prakash would go and Chetan stayed to protect the fields. Raj bought 75 sacks of wheat in the market whereas Om Prakash bought 45 sacks. At home, they split the sacks equally. Chetan had paid 1400 Rupess for the wheat. How much money did Raj and Om Prakash get from the sum, considering equal split of the sacks?

Riddle No. 149

What do the numbers 11, 69 and 88 all have in common?

Riddle No. 150

I have as many brothers as sisters, but my brothers have twice the number of sisters as brothers. How many of us are there?

Riddle No. 151

Two friends were leaving the restaurant and as they passed the cashier. One of them paid his bill, but the other handed the cashier a slip of paper with the number 1004180 written on it. The cashier studied the number for a moment, and then let the friend pass by without paying. Why?

Riddle No. 152

After the autumn harvest, there were nine ears of corn left in the farmer's field. Each night a hungry rabbit sneaked into the field and took three ears home with him. How many nights did it take to get all the corn?

Riddle No. 153

A donkey was tied to a rope six feet long. A bale of hay was 18 feet away and the donkey wanted to eat the hay. How could he do it?

Riddle No. 154

I drive at an average speed of 30 miles per hour to the metro station each morning to catch my train. On a particular morning there was a lot of traffic and at the halfway point I found I had averaged only 15 miles per hour. How fast must I drive for the rest of the way to catch my train?

Riddle No. 155

Round as a cup,
Deep as a glass,
Twenty-five elephants,
Cannot lift it up!

Riddle No. 156

My author's uncertain yet my title's the same. I contain random text yet order's my aim. Read me one day and see my pages are totally bare. Try again another day and the words will be there. I'm not a book of magic although it may sound. I can predict the future and inside your life can be found. Move my eye, I become involved in lactic extraction. But that's just a clue, a minor distraction. What am I?

Riddle No. 157

I have no eyes no legs or ears and I help move the earth.

Riddle No. 158

Each morning I appear to lie at your feet. All day I will follow you, no matter how fast you run. Yet I nearly perish in the midday sun.

Riddle No. 159

To cross the water I'm the way. For water I'm above: I touch it not and truth to say I neither swim nor move.

Riddle No. 160

Look in my face I am somebody; look in my back I am nobody.

Riddle No. 161

A box without hinges, key, or lid. But golden treasure inside is hid.

Riddle No. 162

A place with a lot of substance and story;
Where any one can achieve their glory;
A masquerade can be it's term,
Where you can be anything, a tree to a fern. What am I?

Riddle No. 163

In order to go on you need it. In order to leave you must lose it. In order to survive you must protect it. It is doomed by death, cursed from below, yet everything has it. What is it?

Riddle No. 164

It is sometimes white and sometimes black; you turn it on and turn it off. What is it?

Riddle No. 165

What teaches but doesn't talk, speaks but doesn't make a sound, entertains by imagination and reigns when used.

Riddle No. 166

What gets fat without eating and cries when not sad. What gives birth without conceiving and shouts when not mad?

Riddle No. 167

There is something that is nothing, but it has a name. It joins our walks; it joins in our conversations; it plays in every game. What is it?

Riddle No. 168

A boy buys a female mouse from the pet store and brings it home. If one mouse can give birth to 10 mouselets and after a week, those mouselets can give birth to 10 mouselets and after a week, those mouselets can give birth to 10 mouselets... so on and so on. How many mice will the boy have after three months?

Riddle No. 169

If you can touch it, you cannot go in. If you cannot touch it, you can go in. What is it?

Riddle No. 170

At a garden shop they're selling Magic Grass, a patch of sod that doubles in size every day. A man goes to buy some and figures that his garden is big enough that if he buys one patch, it will cover his garden in fourteen days, because each day it doubles in size. So he decides to speed up the process, and buys two patches of sod.

How many days will it now take for the Magic Grass to cover his garden?

Riddle No. 171

Rajeev has been married for ten years and his wife says, 'My anniversary present better be on the driveway tomorrow and it better go from 0-200 in 2 seconds.' A small package shows up for her the next morning. What is it?

Riddle No. 172

Five hundred begins it, five hundred ends it,
Five in the middle is seen;
First of all figures, the first of all letters,
Take up their stations between.
Join all together, and then you will bring;
Before you the name of an eminent king.

Riddle No. 173

It goes in dry and comes out wet. It gets stronger and stronger the longer it stays in. What is it?

Riddle No. 174

Fatherless and motherless; born without sin. Roared when it came into the world and never spoke again.

Riddle No. 175

In the dark night, a many-hued phantom flies. It soars and spreads its wings above the gloomy human crowd. The whole world calls to it; the whole world implores it. At dawn the phantom vanishes to be re-born in every heart. And every night it is born anew and every day it dies! What is it?

Riddle No. 176

When a dragon flies, he seeks it with his eyes. When a dragon roars, he holds it in his claws. When he slumbers deep, he dreams of it in his sleep. But there beneath his head, it forms his stony bed. What is it?

Riddle No. 177

What is lighter than a feather, but the strongest man in the world can't hold it very long?

Riddle No. 178

Almost everyone needs it, asks for it, gives it, but almost nobody takes it. What is it?

ANSWERS

Riddle No. 1

The big Indian is the little Indian's mother.

Riddle No. 2

20 minutes, 4 eggs can be boiled at the same time.

Riddle No. 3

Twelve (12). All of them have at least 28 days.

Riddle No. 4

No. He must be dead if it is his widow.

Riddle No. 5

Seventy (70). Thirty (30) divided by 1/2 is 6.

Riddle No. 6

One hour. If you take the first pill at 1:00, the second at 1:30 and the third at 2:00, the pills have run out and only one hour has passed.

Riddle No. 7

The answer is '5'. The countersign is always the number of letters of the number that the guard gives. ('six' has 3 letters and 'twelve' has 6 letters. After the two soldiers passed, the first spy thought the answer was half of the number that the guard gave (like what you also might have thought), so he answered 5 when the guard said 10, which was wrong as ten has 3 letters).

Riddle No. 8

THE GERMAN.

Riddle No. 9

Happy Birthday!

Riddle No. 10

Nutan's father married the sister of Nutan's husband.

Riddle No. 11

By gradually pouring sand into the hole. The bird will keep moving so that it is not buried in the sand, forcing it higher and higher until it comes out.

Riddle No. 12

Twenty-nine snips. The last two inches are divided by one snip.

Riddle No.13

The man's old password was 'out of date'.
His new password was 'different'.

Riddle No. 14

He was walking.

Riddle No. 15

The word is 'NOWHERE'. When a space is placed between the 'w' and 'h', you get the words 'NOW HERE'.

Riddle No. 16

The woman was a photographer. She shot a picture of her husband, developed it and hung it up to dry.

Riddle No. 17

The Police didn't tell the man where the crime scene was, but the man knew.

Riddle No. 18

SAWDUST.

Riddle No. 19

Number 194.

Riddle No. 20

YOUR NAME.

Riddle No. 21

The vowels (a, e, i, o, u).

Riddle No. 22

The letter V.

Riddle No. 23

Clove/ Glove/ Grove/ Grave/ Grape/ Graph.

Riddle No. 24

Because he is a still living.

Riddle No. 25

The four suits in a deck of standard playing cards
The Spade is a gardener's tool.
The Diamond is the hardest gem to break. 'Little Girl and
Queen' is a Mother Goose rhyme, in which the Queen gave
the girl a large diamond for picking some roses for her.
The Heart bonds with the mind to form love. Absence makes
the heart grow fonder.
The Club, or Clover, is three dots connected around a stem.

Riddle No. 26

It had too many problems.

Riddle No. 27

14 horses and 8 men. 14×4 plus 8×2 = 72 feet.

Riddle No. 28

Example: 26 + 78 + 39 = 131,821,111,415
26: Use its right number as an exponent, then the answer is
64.
78: The same as the 26. Then the answer is 5,782,378
39: The same one. The answer is 19,683
After that, add them all.
The answer is 3,811,145, but this is not finished.
After you add, write in the paper the answer and write: One
3, one 8, three 1's, one 4 and one 5.
Translate in numbers: 1,318,311,415.

Riddle No. 29

The boy runs halfway across the bridge and turns around. The boy looks like he is running to the island and is sent to the mainland.

Riddle No. 30

Because Satish is 5 days older than Jatin!

Riddle No. 31

140 minutes

Riddle No. 32

Ask which door the other troll would point to if you asked which door leads to heaven. The troll who lies will be forced to point to the door that leads to hell and the honest troll would consider the point of view of the dishonest troll and also point towards the door leading to hell.

Riddle No. 33

LOL. $101 \times 5 = 505$ which looks like SOS.

$567 \times 2 = 01134$ (put in calculator and turn upside down) looks like hello

$101 \times 7 = 707$ turn upside down and it becomes LOL.

Riddle No. 34

The glass is getting bigger in height, but smaller in width.

Riddle No. 35

The facts in this riddle are clear: There is an initial ₹3,000 charge. It should have been ₹2,500, so ₹500 must be returned and accounted for. ₹300 is given to the 3 friends, ₹ 200 is kept by the Assistant; there you have the ₹500. The trick to this riddle is that the addition and subtraction are done at the wrong times to misdirect your thinking.

Riddle No. 36

Light one fuse at both ends and, at the same time, light the second fuse at one end. When the first fuse has completely burned, you know that a half hour has elapsed, and, more relevantly, that the second fuse has a half hour left to go. At this time, light the second fuse from the other end. This will cause it to burn out in 15 more minutes. At that point, exactly 45 minutes will have elapsed.

Riddle No. 37

$6 = 3$

$7 = 5$

Because the numbers to the right are the number of letters in the number words.

Riddle No. 38

1.5876 (turn your calculator upside down and spell 0.1134-hello, 14-hi).

Riddle No. 39

7638.

Riddle No. 40

They actually spent ₹2,500 + ₹200 tip = 2,700 and got back ₹100 each which = 3000. In the first equation, the tip is part of the ₹2,700, but then calculated again instead of the ₹3,000 they got as change.

Riddle No. 41

1 MINUTE.

Riddle No. 42

1:11 am, 2:22 am, 3:33 am, 4:44 am, 5:55 am, 10:00 am, 11:10 am, 11:11 am, 11:12 am, 11:13 am, 11:14 am, 11:15 am, 11:16 am, 11:17 am, 11:18 am, 11:19 am, 12:22 am, 1:11 pm, 2:22 pm, 3:33 pm, 4:44 pm, 5:55 pm, 10:00 pm, 11:10 pm, 11:11 pm, 11:12 pm, 11:13 pm, 11:14 pm, 11:15 pm, 11:16 pm, 11:17 pm, 11:18 pm, 11:19 pm, 12:22 pm.

Riddle No. 43

3. You de-code the numbers by telling the bouncer the sum of all the letters. (other examples: four would be four, three would be five and fifty would be five)

Riddle No. 44

A coconut tree.

Riddle No. 45

A: 98

B: 0

C: 1

D: 0

E: 1

It might be expected intuitively that Dacoit A will have to allocate little if any to himself for fear of being shot dead so that there are fewer dacoits to share between. However, this is as far from the theoretical result as is possible.

This is apparent if we work backwards: if all except D and E have been thrown overboard, D proposes 100 for himself and 0 for E. He has the casting vote, and so this is the allocation.

If there are three left (C, D and E) C knows that D will offer E 0 in the next round; therefore, C has to offer E 1 coin in this round to make E vote with him, and get his allocation through. Therefore, when only three are left the allocation is C:99, D:0, E:1.

If B, C, D and E remain, B knows this when he makes his decision. To avoid being thrown overboard, he can simply offer 1 to D. Because he has the casting vote, the support only by D is sufficient. Thus he proposes B:99, C:0, D:1, E:0. One might consider proposing B:99, C:0, D:0, E:1, as E knows he won't get more, if any, if he throws B overboard. But, as each pirate is eager to throw each other overboard, E would prefer to kill B, to get the same amount of gold from C.

Assuming A knows all these things, he can count on C and E's support for the following allocation, which is the final solution.

Riddle No. 46

Because six has 3 letters, 3 has 5, 5 has 4, 4 has 4.

Riddle No. 47

BRASS!
According to the chemical Periodic Table:
35 = Bromine (Br)
33 = Arsenic (As)
16 = Sulphur (S)
35 + 33 + 16 = BRASS!

Riddle No. 48

1113213211 - After the first line, each line describes the previous line. For example, the second line 11 says, there is one 1 in the first line and the third line 21 says, there are two ones (11) in the second line.

Riddle No. 49

Fill the 3-gallon container with oil and pour it into the 5-gallon container. Then fill the 3-gallon container again and use it to fill the 5-gallon container the rest of the way. Out of the 3-gallon oil, 2-gallon will be required to fill the 5-gallon container completely. Hence one gallon will be left in the 3-gallon container.

Riddle No. 50

A Surname.

Riddle No. 51

Five. There are only four colours, so five socks guarantee that two will be the same colour.

Riddle No. 52

No- it does not collapse. Because it has driven a half mile - you would subtract the gas used from the total weight of the truck.

Riddle No. 53

Seven. The four daughters have only one brother, making five children, plus mom and dad.

Riddle No. 54

Queue.

Riddle No. 55

She was a hurricane.

Riddle No. 56

A lie, because the statement itself says that everything told will be a lie.

Riddle No. 57

Letter 'E' is the most commonly used letter in English language, yet in the whole passage, there is no 'E' used.

Riddle No. 58

Vikram said: 'You will boil me in water.' The goblins were faced with a dilemma. If they boil him in water that would make his statement true, which means he should have been fried in oil. They can only fry him in oil if he makes a true statement, but if they do, it would make his final statement false. The fairies had no way out of their situation so they were forced to set Vikram free.

Riddle No. 59

Fill the 3-cup container with milk and then pour all three cups of milk into the 5-cup container. Fill the 3-cup container with milk again and then use it to fill the 5-cup container the rest of the way. The remainder left in the 3 cup container will equal one cup.

Riddle No. 60

There are three possible solutions for this 51 and 15. 42 and 24, 60 and 06.

Riddle No. 61

Take the goat over first and come back. Then take the lion over and bring the goat back. Now take the stack of leaves over and come back alone to get the goat. Take the goat over and the job is done!

Riddle No. 62

You turn 2 switches on and leave 1 switch off and wait about a minute. Then enter the room, but just before you enter, turn one switch from on to off. Once in the room, feel the lightbulb - if it is warm, but off, it has to be the last switch you turned off. If it is on, it has to be the switch left on. If it is cold and is off, it has to be the switch you left in the off position.

Riddle No. 63

The man did exactly as he said he would and wrote 'your exact weight' on the paper.

Riddle No. 64

Draw an S in front of the IX and it spells SIX. No one said the line had to be straight.

Riddle No. 65

What the ant eats.

Riddle No. 66

Concrete floor is too hard to crack due to an egg falling on it.

Riddle No. 67

They are grandmother, mother and daughter.

Riddle No. 68

You light the matchstick first.

Riddle No. 69

Halfway through the woods: After halfway, the dog would be running out of the woods, not into the woods.

Riddle No. 70

Pressure.

Riddle No. 71

It is the only number that has all the digits arranged in alphabetical order.

Riddle No. 72

A and W (and why) - The pattern is the first letter of every word in the sentence.

Riddle No. 73

120 times.

Riddle No. 74

0 ft. The rope sags 500 ft from the top of the post to make it 250 ft above the ground. Since the rope is 1000 ft, it must be folded directly in half, which would happen only if the two posts were right next to each other.

Riddle No. 75

The third—Lions that have not eaten in three years are dead.

Riddle No. 76

A wheelbarrow.

Riddle No. 77

Everything in the MAGIC WORLD must contain double letters in each word.

Riddle No. 78

The Moon.

Riddle No. 79

How about—one word.

Riddle No. 80

Neither. The yolk of the egg is yellow.

Riddle No. 81

Ear.

Riddle No. 82

One in six. A dice has no memory of what it last showed.

Riddle No. 83

Memories.

Riddle No. 84

None. Cows cannot talk!

Riddle No. 85

Yesterday, today and tomorrow

Riddle No. 86

87—he's looking at the numbers upside down.

Riddle No. 87

Nothing.

Riddle No. 88

No

Explanation: While many people argue that the answer to the riddle is Pressure, the fact of the matter is that the only question that has been asked in the riddle is, can you answer this riddle.

Riddle No. 89

The man should ask the stranger the way back to his own village; the stranger from the village of Liars will take him to the village of Truths and the stranger from the village of Truths, will take him to the village of Truths.

Riddle No. 90

The two words are:
Outgoing and retiring.

Riddle No. 91

A chicken cannot talk.

Riddle No. 92

His house is a boat in the middle of the sea.

Riddle No. 93

A coin.

Riddle No. 94

Lightning.

Riddle No. 95

It states, 'There are only three words in *the English language*. What is the third word?' The third word of that phrase is of course 'language'. Don't get angry at me!! :)

Riddle No. 96

A coffin.

Riddle No. 97

Bookkeeper: An alternate, tricky, answer could be Woollen (where W is a 'double u').

Riddle No. 98

Charcoal.

Riddle No. 99

Fire.

Riddle No. 100

A frog: The frog is an amphibian in the order Anura (meaning 'tail-less') and usually makes noises at night during its mating season.

Riddle No. 101

Senselessness.

Riddle No. 102

The year is read the same upside down as rightside up. (6009).

Riddle No. 103

AGE.

Riddle No. 104

Someone's age.

Riddle No. 105

35 customers. The numbers reversed are 31415926 and with a decimal they are 3.1415926, which is Pi, meaning the next number is 53, reversed to be 35.

Riddle No. 106

Typewriter.

Riddle No. 107

It can be either tomorrow or the future. Once it's here it is no longer tomorrow, but today. It's no longer the future, but the present.

Riddle No. 108

A candle.

Riddle No. 109

Sands in an hourglass.

Riddle No. 110

Electricity (or lightning).

Riddle No. 111

A deciduous tree.

Riddle No. 112

An ace (in a deck of cards).

Riddle No. 113

The letter: D.

Riddle No. 114

A Tower.

Riddle No. 115

A thorn.

Riddle No. 116

The hands on a clock: (hour, minute, second).

Riddle No. 117

The letter: S.

Riddle No. 118

Important.

Riddle No. 119

Gravity.

Riddle No. 120

Dog: Dog days, hot dog, dog pound, dog fight.

Riddle No. 121

Wednesday.
The Sun of the alpha position where $A = 1, B = 2, C = 3$, etc...

Riddle No. 122

A smile.

Riddle No. 123

The four suits in a deck of standard playing cards.
The Spade is a gardener's tool.
The Diamond is the hardest gem to break. 'Little Girl and Queen' is a Mother Goose rhyme, in which the Queen gave

the girl a large diamond for picking some roses for the Queen. The Heart bonds with the mind to form love. Absence makes the heart grow fonder.

The Club, or Clover, is three dots connected around a stem.

Riddle No. 124

A rainbow.

Riddle No. 125

Scent, cent, sent.

Riddle No. 126

Wheat / Heat/ Eat/ Tea.

Riddle No. 127

Princes.

Riddle No. 128

Spice, Ice, 1°C.

Riddle No. 129

A fish.

Riddle No. 130

A mountain (from Tolkien).

Riddle No. 131

The horse's name is Friday.

Riddle No. 132

Darkness.

Riddle No. 133

The sun shining on daisies.

Riddle No. 134

Anjali.

Riddle No. 135

Heroine (he, her, hero).

Riddle No. 136

Andrew.

Riddle No. 137

Wise you are, wise you be, I see you are too wise for *me*.

Riddle No. 138

Pi (3.141592653).

Riddle No. 139

Moths.

Explanation: Most species of moths are nocturnal, yet they are attracted to light and can be found in homes. Men, in the most generic sense, can be scared of moths (Mottephobia) as well as the damage they can cause as pests to bee hives, grain, flour, trees and agriculture. Women like moths because of the silk they produce. Children frequently chase and play with moths. Moths are attracted to salt and love to eat rotting fruit (such as dates). Some species of moths are densely covered with tiny hairs and of course it starts with the letter 'm'. Lastly, moths are mentioned in the Quran (*101:4 (Asad) [It will occur] on the Day when men will be like moths swarming in confusion*).

Riddle No. 140

Four orphaned siblings.

Riddle No. 141

A circle.

Riddle No. 142

A pencil.

Riddle No. 143

The key to this math riddle is realising that the one place must be zero.

$888 + 88 + 8 + 8 + 8 = 1,000$

Riddle No. 144

The answer is 4.

77. The subsequent numbers are obtained by multiplying together the digits of the previous one—

$7 \times 7 = 49; 4 \times 9 = 36$

Riddle No. 145

One of the 'fathers' is also a grandfather. Therefore, the other father is both a son and a father to the grandson. In other words, the one father is both a son and a father.

Riddle No. 146

11 cartons total.
7 large boxes ($7 \times 8 = 56$ boxes)
4 small boxes ($4 \times 10 = 40$ boxes)
11 total cartons and 96 boxes.

Riddle No. 147

Post Office.

Riddle No. 148

Every farmer's part is $1/3(45+75) = 40$ sacks.
Chetan paid ₹1400 for 40 sacks, then 1 sack costs
₹1400/40 = ₹35/sack.
Raj got ₹35 (45-40) = 35×5 = ₹175.
Om Prakash got ₹35 (75–40) = 35×35 = ₹1225.
Answer: Om Prakash ₹1225, Raj ₹175.

Riddle No. 149

They read the same backwards and forward.

Riddle No. 150

Seven. The only possible solution is that the person talking
is a woman and there are four women and three men.

Riddle No. 151

The number 1004180: I owe nothing, for I ate nothing.

Riddle No. 152

Nine nights. Two of the ears belonged to the rabbit.

Riddle No. 153

Very easily as the rope wasn't tied to anything.

Riddle No. 154

The train is just about to leave the station and there is no way I will be able to catch it this time.

Riddle No. 155

There are several answers.
One potential answer is: 31 quarters, 21 dimes, 3 nickels, and 0 pennies.

Riddle No. 156

A diary.

Riddle No. 157

A worm.

Riddle No. 158

I am your shadow.

Riddle No. 159

I am a bridge to help you cross.

Riddle No. 160

I am a mirror.

Riddle No. 161

AN EGG

Riddle No. 162

A stage.

Riddle No. 163

Life.

Riddle No. 164

A light bulb.

Riddle No. 165

A book.

Riddle No. 166

Clouds.

Riddle No. 167

Our shadow.

Riddle No. 168

You can't make a mouselet with only one mouse!

Riddle No. 169

Your coffin.

Riddle No. 170

13.

Riddle No. 171

A scale.

Riddle No. 172

DAVID (Roman numerals).

Riddle No. 173

It's not what you think. It's only a tea bag.

Riddle No. 174

Thunder.

Riddle No. 175

Hope or dreams.

Riddle No. 176

Jewels, gems, treasure, etc.

Riddle No. 177

His breath.

Riddle No. 178

Advice.

www.ingramcontent.com/pod-product-compliance
Lightning Source LLC
Chambersburg PA
CBHW031209260626
47169CB00004B/1297